Handbook of
Bansuri

HISTORY | *ANATOMY* | *TUNING* | *MAINTENANCE*

Handbook of
Bansuri

HISTORY | ANATOMY | TUNING | MAINTENANCE

By

Pankaj Vishal

PANKAJ PUBLICATIONS
New Delhi, INDIA

Handbook of Bansuri
First Published May, 2008
Copyright © Pankaj Publications

ISBN 13 :978-81-87155-99-7
ISBN 10 :81-87155-99-X

Published by :
PANKAJ PUBLICATION
M-114, Vikas Puri
New Delhi 110 018
Email : *contact@pankajmusic.com*
 www.pankajmusic.com

For bulk purchases and business inquiries,
contact@pankajmusic.com

Cover design by	:	Square vision
Typesetting by	:	Pankaj Books
Illustrations by	:	Mohit Suneja
Printed in India by	:	

Preface

The tradition of music in our country is as old as the civilization of this country itself. It is often said that the Lord created the entire universe and kept it moving with the effect of 'Maya'. When ever the Lord played His flute, the 'Maya' got going.

The name of Bansuri is attached to the creator of this universe itself. It is so old and so lucky that the Lord found it worth keeping it over His lips.

Even if one does not agree with the divinity of the Bansuri, one would hardly disagree about it's soothing and satiating effect, which takes the listeners on the sojourn of the unseen.

With this in mind, we would like to introduce to the readers with one of the most important instruments of Indian Musical Tradition - the Bansuri. This book gives a sound idea of the history, development and basics of the instrument, to begin with and facilitates the reader in motivating his interest to know more about this wonderful instrument for further learning.

This book takes care of the inquisitiveness of beginners and points out the salient probable problem areas of this field in a friendly manner.

Any suggestion for improvement of this book is welcome.

PANKAJ VISHAL

Publishers' Note

The PANKAJ PUBLICATIONS is an undisputed leader and pioneer in the field of music books. The house is in continuous service to music lovers spread all over the world by promoting Indian music religiously by way of its books, C.D.s, journals and assisting practicing musicians.

A series of books with vital information about the musical instruments, its origin, evolution, playing technique, etc. was in great demand for the last couple of years. In view of the larger interest of readers in general and music lovers in particular, we have brought this series of 'Handbooks' at the lowest possible price.

The entire editorial team of the PANKAJ PUBLICATIONS carried out intensive research and came out with fruits in the form of these books. We hope this series will be of immense help to people as our previous series of 'Pankaj Learn to play' proved to be.

If we are successful in our mission, although in a little way, the entire team along with this publication will be proud of the effort.

- *PUBLISHER*

Contents

ఠ ━━━━━━━━━━━━━━━━━━━━━━━━━━ ౧

Part - 1
Theory of Music

The Indian Music System

Indian Music is based on *Ragas* and *Ragas* are based on *the Nadas, Shrutis, Swaras, Saptaka* and *Thaats*, as shown in the evolution chart.

Nada (Sound) : This is sound produced by striking, friction or beating. *'Nada'* is of two kinds:

(a) *Sangeet-un-upyogi Nada* **(Non-Musical sound)**: Those sounds which are not musical such as machine rattlings, traffic horns, shouting etc. These sounds are not pleasant to listen to and are disturbing in nature. They can cause headaches and irritation. We hear these sounds in our day-to-day lives in the city.

(b) *Sangeet-upyogi Nada* **(Musical sound):** Contrary to non-musical sounds, these sounds are pleasant to listen to and musically audible. These can be the sounds of nature as the chirping of birds, water falls, flowing river, singing etc. These sounds are relaxing and give a feeling of tranquility and peace. Musical sounds like singing and instrumental playing have the virtue to hypnotize an audience.

Shruti **(Microtonal Interval notes)**: These are microtonal sounds found between ***Sangeet-upyogi Nadas*** (musical sounds). They can be heard and distinguished by a sensitive musical ear only. They can now be seen visually on an 'Oscilloscope'. *Shrutis* are also called Microtonal Intervals of Sound. The gaps are increased between the sounds to make these **Shrutis** to **notes** for the purpose of easy recognition and the development of music by using them when playing and singing.

There are 22 *Shrutis* used in Indian Music.

1. Tivra	8. Raudri	15. Rakta
2. Kumudwati	9. Krodhi	16. Sandipini
3. Manda	10. Vajrika	17. Alapini
4. Chhandovati	11. Prasarini	18. Madanti
5. Dayawati	12. Priti	19. Rohini
6. Ranjani	13. Manjari	20. Romya
7. Raktika	14. Kshiti	21. Ugra
		22. Kshobhini

Swaras (Notes): *Swaras* (notes) are produced by *Shrutis* with big intervals or Gaps. They can be distinguished by the ears of listeners. The difference between 'Swaras' and 'Shrutis' is that the 'Swaras' are measured by *Shrutis* depending on the intervals or number of *Shrutis*.

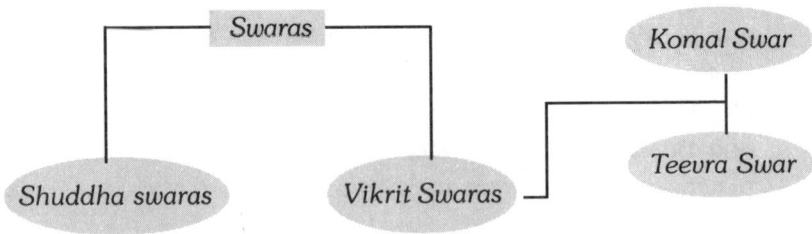

Swaras are of two types, *Vikrits* **Swara (Distorted note)** and **Shuddha Swara (Full Tone note)**

Shuddha Swaras (Full Tone Notes). These are natural notes which are found in the *Shrutis*. To recognize the minute gap of *Shrutis* easily.

Shudha Swaras or Full Tone Notes were identified and called **Natural notes** and they are 7 of them.

Vedic names along with the popular short names of these 7 notes are given below. The complete music theory is based on these 7 notes and their combinations.

S. No.	Name of Swaras	Shuddha Swaras	Western Notes	Shruti
1.	Shadaj	Sa	C	4 Tivra, Kumudwati, Manda Chhandovati.
2.	Rishabh	Re	D	3 Dayawati, Ranjani, Raktika
3.	Gandhar	Ga	E	2 Raudri & Krodhi
4.	Madhyam	Ma	F	4 Vajrika, Prasarini, Priti, Manjari
5.	Pancham	Pa	G	4 Kshiti, Rakta, Sandipini Alapini
6.	Dhaiwat	Dha	A	3 Madanti, Rohini, Romya
7.	Nishad	Ni	B	2 Ugra Kshobhini

With the identification of these full tone notes the gap between the notes becomes wider. The wider the gap the greater the obstruction to the sweetness of sound. Musicians then introduced **Half Tone Notes** or **Flat Notes** (*Komal Swaras*) between two **Full Tone Notes** (*Shuddha Swaras*), and thus **Distorted notes** (*Vikrit Swaras*) came into existance.

Vikrit Swaras **(Distorted Notes)** : *Vikrit Swara*s are of two types, they are *Komal Swara*s (Flat Notes or Half Tone Notes) and *Tivra Swara* (Sharp note). With the introduction of the distorted notes, *Sa* and *Pa* though remained unchanged.

Komal Swaras **(Flat notes or Half Tone Notes)** are found between two **shudha swaras (Full Tone notes)**. These *Swara*s are a bit lower in pitch from the *Shuddha Swara*s. They are symbolized in notation by a Dash (_) below the note such as **Re**. A half step lower.

✌ There are four *Komal Swara*s (flat notes). These are: **Re, Ga, Dha, & Ni**.

Tivra Swar is the note which appears a half step above the full note and is called a **sharp note (*Tivra Swar*)**. This *Swar* (note) is higher in pitch from the *Shuddha Swara*. It is symbolized in notation by a small vertical line (ˈ) over the note.

✌ There is only one *Tivra Swar,* which is **Ma**.

According to two different notation systems, it is important to understand the difference between the two. There are two fixed notes in Indian system. These are **Sa** & **Pa**. The remaining five notes have two different types as semitone or distorted forms. On the other hand there are two types for all the seven notes in the western system. There is a distortion of each note and all the notes can be either flat or sharp. The closest related western note to the Indian distorted notes are as follows -

Indian Notes	Re	Ga	Ma	Dha	Ni
Western Notes	C# or D♭	D# or E♭	F# or G♭	G# or A♭	A# or B♭

1. As shown in the table, note **komal Re** is shown as it is but in western system, it is written as two types, either **C#** or **D♭**. Where (**#**) symbol is used for sharp (*tivra*) and (♭) symbol is used for flat (*komal*).

2. There are two fixed notes in the Indian system. These are **Sa** & **Pa**, which cannot be changed to flats or sharp.

3. Western music does not have sharp for note **E** & **B**. Instead, **F** stands for **E#**, and **C** stands for **B#**.

This is how the Twelve notes come to exist. They are as follows.

Sl. No.	Swaras	Description	Western Name
1.	**Sa**	*Shudha* (Fixed)	**C Fixed**
2.	<u>Re</u>	*Komal*	D Half Tone note
3.	**Re**	*Shuddha*	**D Full tone note**
4.	<u>Ga</u>	*Komal*	E Half tone note
5.	**Ga**	*Shuddha*	**E Full tone note**
6.	**Ma**	*Shudha*	**F Full tone note**
7.	Ma'	*Tivra*	F Sharp note
8.	**Pa**	*Shuddha* (Fixed)	**G Fixed**
9.	<u>Dha</u>	*Komal*	A Half tone note
10.	**Dha**	*Shuddha*	**A Full note**
11.	<u>Ni</u>	*Komal*	B Half Tone note
12.	**Ni**	*Shuddha*	**B Full Note**

A group of these 7 Natural Notes (*Shuddha Swaras*) make a *Saptak* (Octave). The *Saptak* also includes 4 *Komal* and one *Tivra Swar*. In all there are 12 Notes to make a complete **Saptak (Octave).** A *Saptak* (Octave) includes the *guru* notes of Indian Music which are **Sa Re Ga Ma Pa Dha Ni.** A specific combination of these *Swar*as (Notes) from the *Saptak* forms a **Thaat (scale)**, which is the basis of the *Ragas*.

Ragas (Melodies) are a particular combination of these notes or group of notes, which are produced from **Thaats (scales)**.

In a nutshell, we can understand the journey of swaras from its origin to Nada by this evolution chart.

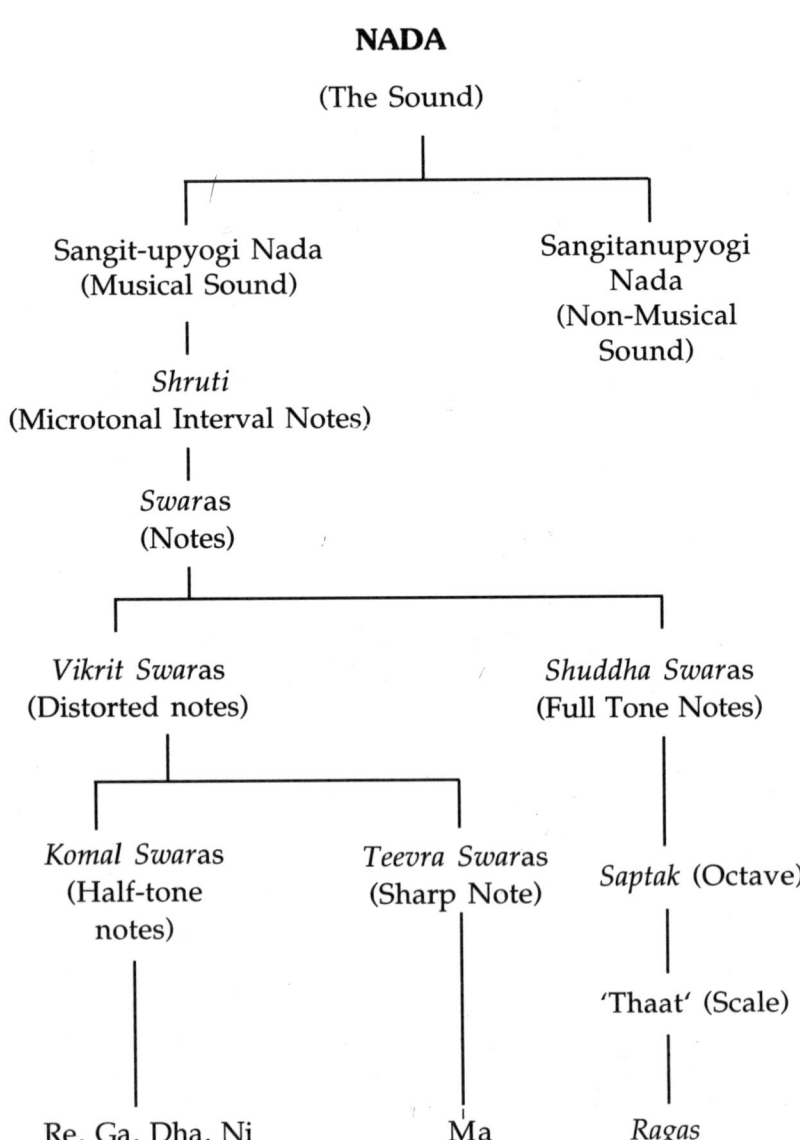

NADA

(The Sound)

Sangit-upyogi Nada
(Musical Sound)

Sangitanupyogi
Nada
(Non-Musical
Sound)

Shruti
(Microtonal Interval Notes)

Swaras
(Notes)

Vikrit Swaras
(Distorted notes)

Shuddha Swaras
(Full Tone Notes)

Komal Swaras
(Half-tone
notes)

Teevra Swaras
(Sharp Note)

Saptak (Octave)

'Thaat' (Scale)

Re, Ga, Dha, Ni

Ma

Ragas
(Melodies)

SAPTAK (Octave)

According to the Indian theory of music there are three ranges of the human voice, which are low, medium and high pitch. These pitches when identified with notes in music called *Saptaka* or a group of seven *Shuddha* notes. These seven notes also includes four *komal* and one *Tivra Swara*. The human voice is differentiated under these three ranges:

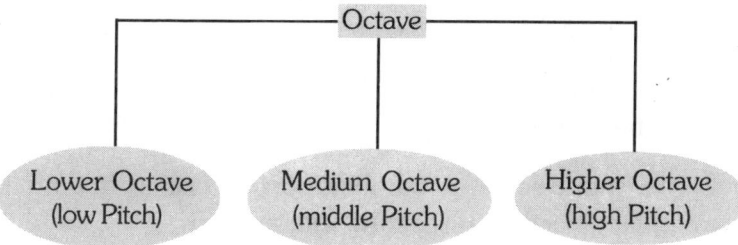

1. ***Madhya Saptaka*** (Medium Octave) — When the sound naturally comes out of the throat without any pressure, it is called the throat voice. The Medium octave or *Madhya Saptaka*.

2. ***Mandra Saptaka*** (Lower Octave) — When the sound comes out entirely by the pressure of the lungs, it is called the chest voice or *Mandra Saptaka* (Lower Octave). In this *Saptaka* the pitch of the sound is lower than the medium octave.

3. ***Tar Saptaka*** (Upper Octave) — When the sound is produced with the exertion of force on the nostrils and head, called the head voice or *Tar Saptaka* (Upper Octave). The pitch or sound is higher than that of the medium octave.

THAAT

Ordinarily a *Thaat* is a combination of **seven Swaras** or notes capable of producing *Ragas*. All the notes played in *thaat* are in ascending order starting from **Sa** ending at **Ni,** whether natural, flat or sharp. There are basically ten *thaats* in Indian music system.

The *Thaat* must qualify these three Basic conditions :

1. A *Thaat* must contain the seven *swaras* (notes) in the regular form.

2. The *Shuddha, Komal* or *Tivra Swaras* must appear one after the other.

3. It is a mere scale, a combination of notes. It does not essentially need to please the listeners ear.

Ten thaats and their notes as follows:

1.	Bilawal	Sa	Re	Ga	Ma	Pa	Dha	Ni
2.	Khamaj	Sa	Re	Ga	Ma	Pa	Dha	<u>Ni</u>
3.	Kafee	Sa	Re	<u>Ga</u>	Ma	Pa	Dha	<u>Ni</u>
4.	Asawari	Sa	Re	<u>Ga</u>	Ma	Pa	<u>Dha</u>	<u>Ni</u>
5.	Bhairav	Sa	<u>Re</u>	Ga	Ma	Pa	<u>Dha</u>	Ni
6.	Kalyan	Sa	Re	Ga	Ma'	Pa	Dha	Ni
7.	Poorvi	Sa	<u>Re</u>	Ga	Ma	Pa	<u>Dha</u>	Ni
8.	Bhairavi	Sa	<u>Re</u>	<u>Ga</u>	Ma	Pa	<u>Dha</u>	<u>Ni</u>
9.	Todi	Sa	<u>Re</u>	<u>Ga</u>	Ma'	Pa	<u>Dha</u>	Ni
10.	Marva	Sa	<u>Re</u>	Ga	Ma	Pa	Dha	Ni

RAGAS

A *Raga* is a combination of sounds or *swaras* having qualities that give pleasure to the listener. Every *Raga* has a peculiar quality of its own. To be acquainted with *Ragas*, a musician should bear in mind the following points :

1. *Ragas* must belong to a *Thaat*.

2. At least five notes are essential for a *Raga*.

3. In a *Raga* the melody is very essential.

4. A *Raga* must have its own ascent, descent (*Aroha* and *avaroha*) and fixed notes *(Vadi & Samvadi)*.

5. The **Sa** *Swara* (C note) is the same note (fixed) in every *Raga*, and both **Ma** & **Pa** are not to be omitted at the same time.

Parts of combination of a raga

There are 4 distinguished parts of a raga/composition/song.

1. *Sthayi* : First part (face) or introduction.

2. *Antara* : Second part or body.

3. *Sanchari* : Combinarion of notes of 'Sthayi' & 'Antara'.

4. *Abhog* : Some notes of the composition played in the upper octave.

Categories of Ragas (*Jati' of a Raga*)

The following are the three most common categories of Ragas :

1. **Sampurna** has seven notes ascending and descending.

2. **Shadava** has six notes ascending and descending.

3. **Odava** has five notes in the same *Swaras*, both ascending & descending.

Categories of Ragas

S. No.	Category	No. of Swaras		Total No. of Ragas with the Combination of Ascending & Descending Notes
		Ascent	Descent	
1.	Sampurna–Sampurna	7	7	1 – 1 x 1 – 1
2.	Shadava–Shadava	6	6	6 – 6 x 6 – 36
3.	Odava–Odava	5	5	15 – 15x15– 225
4.	Sampurna–Shadava	7	6	6 – 1 x 6 – 6
5.	Sampurna–Odava	7	5	15 – 1 x 15 – 15
6.	Shadva–Sampurna	6	7	6 – 6 x 1 – 6
7.	Shadva–Odava	6	5	90 – 6 x 15 – 90
8.	Odava–Sampurna	5	7	15 – 15 x 1 – 15
9.	Odava–Shadava	5	6	90 – 15 x 6 – 90

Lay (Tempo or Speed)

LAY : (Tempo)

In the ordinary sense **lay** means Beat or speed or any regular space of time between boundaries to complete a circle in a specific time period. It is a natural harmonious flow of vocal and instrumental sound with a regular succession of accents. There is no fixed structure of speed or tempo in music. Every musician chooses it according to his convenience; but basically, what is important is that one should be able to control the *lay* or tempo of *taal*. The tempo should neither be too slow nor should it be extraordinarily fast. Not only this, even in a slow tempo it should be in such a manner that it can entertain the audience on the one hand and on the other its musicality will not be sacrificed.

Normally a slow tempo should be half the tempo of a standard one and a fast tempo should be double that of the standard. But again it differs according to the capabilitiy of the musician. An expert musician starts the tempo in a very slow pace and gradually increases it reaching the required speed.

According to observations there are mainly three types of beat which have been accepted in the Indian music. But there is one more special type called '*Ati Drut Lay*', which is generally used by expert musicians, because tempo in this particular type is very fast and very tough to control. All percussion instruments are used to control and regularize the musical sound.

21

The Three types of beats are :

1. **Madhya Lay** (Medium or Normal Beat).
   eg. 1 2 3 4

2. **Drut Lay** (Quick or Fast Beat).
   eg. 1 2 3 4

3. **Vilambit Lay** (Slow Beat).
   eg. 1   2   3   4

(Note the space between the numbers)

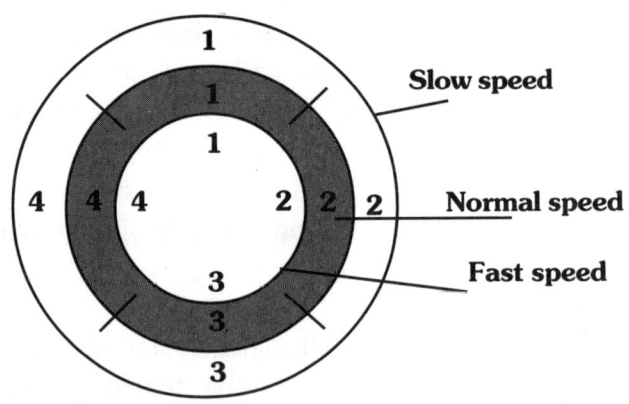

Normal Tempo

Normal Beat is the time required by a musician to complete a round or a part of a song, tune or dance in a comfortable speed without any stress. Although no fix structure is available for this, convenience is the key. The tempo should be easy enough within the musician's control. In a normal speed any composition whether instrumental or vocal leaves a very refreshing effect on the audience. The Normal beat is the basis of the remaining two beats.

Eg. 1 2 3 4 1 2 3 4 etc.

Fast Tempo

Fast Beat means half the time of a normal beat. This is when a musician, say, requires one minute of time to complete a part of a song, tune or dance, in normal beat, now he will require half the time taken by the normal beat. In other words we can say that the musician can take two rounds of his play for the time required in the normal beat.

Eg. 1 2 3 4-1 2 3 4-1 2 3 4 etc.

Slow Tempo

In Slow Beat a musician takes double the time to complete the round required by the medium or normal beat. Suppose if he completes a round of his song in one minute in normal beat, he will now take two minutes to complete the same song.

Eg. 1 - 2 - 3 - 4 - 1 - 2 - 3 - 4   etc.

Comparative speeds in various beats:

Slow beat	: 1		2		3		4	
Medium Beat	: 1	2	3	4	1	2	3	4
Fast Beat	: 1 2 3 4	1 2 3 4	1 2 3 4	1 2 3 4				

Taal (The Rhythm)

Taal or Rhythm is the regular succession of sound vibrations, necessary to make sound musical. It is a scale for producing the rhythmic pattern in a song or *Raga*. Each song or composition runs on a particular time scale, and the scale is repeated in a particular gap, this gap is repeated for a specific number of times, which makes the rhythm cycle for the composition. The gaps between the notes in a scale is known as intervals, which can be created by clapping, or by a percussion instrument. The most popular is the Tabla. The early Indian musicians invented many *taals* of different *matras* (Rhythms), *Khand* (Bars) and *Bols* (Sounds) and fixed the points of *'Sam'*, *Talis* and *Khalis* for every *Taal*.

Beat : As we know well now, beat is a time-scale map in a composition. The common beats in the Indian system are *Kehrava Taal* (8 beats) and *Daadara taal* (6 beats).

Beat and its part in a composition is written and understood by some technical names like *sam, tali, khali,* etc. in the Indian music system. These terms and names carry a lot of importance for the beginners to understand. Let's learn them in detail.

Bol (Sounds) : Each beat is made out of notes or sounds. These sounds can be of percussions or of melody notes. The sounds created by percussions like drums or tabla, played as accompaniment or are spoken as **Dha, Dhin,** etc. are known as Bols.

Sam : The starting point of a taal notation or a beat cycle, from the point where the beat starts in a composition is known as **Sam.** This is the point in a notation where all the instruments stops and start together when playing many instruments together. It is shown in the notation with **(x)** sign.

Taali : Literally means the clap, it is the particular point in a notation where maximum pressure is given to the playing. This is also the repeated starting point of a part in a beat cycle.

For example; as shown below, while playing *"Teen Taal"* 1st, 5th, & 13th bol has *taali* in its place -

Beat signs	×				2			
Beat	1	2	3	4	5	6	7	8
Bol	Dha	Dhin	Dhin	Dha	Dha	Dhin	Dhin	Dha
Beat signs	0				3			
Beat	9	10	11	12	13	14	15	16
Bol	Dha	Tin	Tin	Ta	Ta	Dhin	Dhin	Dha

Khali : Khali literally means empty space, which is actually not, only the force or emphasis of sound is less in this part. *Khali* in a composition means a gap of some *matras* within *boles* of *Theka* played by the right hand on the Tabla only while the left (*Duggi* or *Dhama*) remains silent in *khali matra* time. This is a point in a notation where comparatively less force is given to the *bol*. For example, while playing *"teen taal"*, the 9th beat in the cycle is the space for *khali*.

Parts: Putting all the sounds in a group separated by *sam*, *tali* and *khali* are known as parts or measures. Parts are shown in notation by a vertical line between the group of notes or sounds. For example: *Daadra taal* is of two parts with 3 sounds per measure:

Beat signs	×			0		
Beat	1	2	3	4	5	6
Bol	Dha	Dhin	Na	Ta	Tin	Na

All the symbols such as *sam, tali khali* are placed on the 1st note of the group.

Sthayi : First part or the introduction of the song or a composition which is repeated in the song after paragraphs is called *sthayi*.

Antara : The second part or the middle part of the song which is also known as the body is called *Antara*.

Some Important Beats

Keherva Taal

It is the most popular and common *Taal* used in Indian Light Music. It has 8 '*matras*' or beat with **sam** on the 1st beat and **khali** on the 5th. *Ghazal* and *Bhajan* & Light music get beautiful expression in this *taal*. This *taal* is relatively easy to learn and understand and therefore very popular among musicians.

Parts/Measures - 2   Beats - 8
one taali & one Khali

Beat signs	x				0			
Beat	1	2	3	4	5	6	7	8
Bol	Dha	Ge	Na	Ti	Na	Ka	Dhi	Na

Dadra Taal

This is another popular *taal* of Indian Light Music. It consists of 6 *matras* with *sam* on the 1st and *khali* on 5th. Any composition of '*Sringar Ras*' will suit this *taal*. Generally *Thumri*, *Bhajans* and *Ghazals* are sung in this *taal*. This *taal* is very easy to grasp and learn, therefore it is very much in use in the field of music.

Parts/Measures - 2   Beats - 6
one taali & one Khali

Beat signs	×			0		
Beat	1	2	3	4	5	6
Bol	Dha	Dhin	Na	Dha	Tin	Na

Roopak Taal

One of the most popular *taals* of Indian Music; used both in light as well as classical music. It has 7 beats with *sam* on the 1st and *taali* on 5th & 7th *matras*. Some musicians believe that *khali* is on the 1st. Classical compositions as well as light *bhajans* and *ghazals* are made to flourish in this *taal* very extensively. Being a *taal* of odd numbers it is very impulsive and its least numbers of beat make it easier to grasp and control.

Parts/Measures - 3　　　　　　　　　　*Beats - 7*
Two taali & one Khali

Beat signs	×			2		3	
Beat	1	2	3	4	5	6	7
Bol	Tin	Tin	Na	Dhin	Na	Dhin	Na

(**Note :** Roopak taal starts from sam, so the taali is not given there.)

Deep Chandi Taal

This *taal* is usually used in classical music only. It has 14 beats with *sam* on the 1st. This *taal* is generally used by expert musicians. Although light composition can be sung or played in this *taal* but it is not so easy to handle. Medium tempo compositions are used in this *taal*.

Parts/Measures - 4　　　　　　　　　　*Beats - 14*
Three taali & one Khali

Beat signs	×			2			
Beat	1	2	3	4	5	6	7
Bol	Dha	Dhin	S	Dha	Dha	Tin	S
Beat signs	0			3			
Beat	8	9	10	11	12	13	14
Bol	Ta	Tin	S	Dha	Dha	Dhin	S

Teen Taal

This is the base of all *taals* in Indian Music. It has 16 beats with *sam* on 1st, 2nd taali on 5th, *khali* on 9th and 3rd *taali* on 13th. It is called base of all taals because every other *taal* is in the fraction of *teen taal*. It is easy to learn and most widely used in music both light and classical. Slow and medium and fast compositions are played and sung in this *taal*.

Parts/Measures - 4   *Beats* - 16
Three taali & one Khali

Beat signs	×				2			
Beat	1	2	3	4	5	6	7	8
Bol	Dha	Dhin	Dhin	Dha	Dha	Dhin	Dhin	Dha
Beat signs	0				3			
Beat	9	10	11	12	13	14	15	16
Bol	Dha	Tin	Tin	Ta	Ta	Dhin	Dhin	Dha

Jhap Taal

This *taal* too is very popular but mostly used in classical music. it has 10 matras with *sam* on 1st and 2nd *taali* on 5th, *khali* on 9th and 3rd taali on 10th. Composition in slow and medium tempo is generally used in this *taal*. Although light compositions can be made in this *taal* but generally it is not because its rhythm pattern is somewhat different and not so easy to learn and grasp compared to other *taals*.

Parts/Measures - 4   *Beats* - 10
Three taali & one Khali

Beat signs	×		2		0			3		
Beat	1	2	3	4	5	6	7	8	9	10
Bol	Dhin	Na	Dhin	Dhin	Na	Tin	Na	Dhin	Dhin	Na

Ek Taal

One of the popular *taals* of Indian music system. This *taal* is used in classical music but may be used in light music also. It has 12 *matras* with *sam* on the 1st beat. Slow and fast tempo compositions are used in this *taal*. This *taal* has three times the beat that of *Dadra taal* and hence its rhythm pattern is similar to the later. This *taal* is easy to learn and grasp and is impulsive in nature.

Parts/Measures - 6   *Beats - 12*
Four taali & Two Khali

Beat signs	×		0		2	
Beat	1	2	3	4	5	6
Bol	Dhin	Dhin	DhaGe	TirKit	Tu	Na
Beat signs	0		3		4	
Beat	7	8	9	10	11	12
Bol	Kat	Ta	DhaGe	TirKit	Dhin	Na

Teevra Taal

It is also a popular and old *taal* of Indian music system. Initially it was played on pakhawaj only but now it is widely played in tabla also. Similar to *Roopak* this *taal* has 7 beats. This *taal* is used in classical music only in medium or slow tempo. Its nature is very intense and therefore is used in serious music such as *Dhrupad* and *khayal* etc.

Parts/Measures - 3   *Beats - 7*
Three taali

Beat signs	×			2		3	
Beat	1	2	3	4	5	6	7
Bol	Dha	Din	Ta	Tit	Kat	GaDe	Gin

Indian Music Notation System

Tips to Read a Composition

1. **Shudha Swaras (Full tone Notes):** No sign is required i.e. Sa. Re, Ga, Ma, Pa, Dha, Ni. Only the first letter is required in the notation i.e. S, R, G, M, P, D, N.

2. **Komal Swaras (Half Tone Notes):** A dash (—) is written under the notes i.e. R G D N.

3. **Tivra Swara (Sharp Note):** A small perpendicular line is placed over the note i.e. Ḿ.

4. **Madhya Saptak Swaras (Medium Octave Notes):** No sign is required for this octave notes i.e. S R G M P D N.

5. **Mandra Saptak Swaras (Lower Octave Notes):** A dot is written under the notes i.e. S R G M P D N

6. **Ati Mandra Saptak Swaras (Double lower octave):** Two dots are written under the notes i.e. S P

7. **Tar Saptak Swaras (Upper Octave Notes):** A dot is written over the notes S R G M P D N

8. **Matras** are shown in numbers 1 2 3 4 5 6 etc. Normally one note shows one *Matra* time.

9. **Tali:** Numbers written between the bars.

10. **Khali:** A Zero (0) is shown in a bar.

11. **Sam:** A sign of (×) is written on the first matra of every *Taal*.

12. **Khand (Bar):** Vertical lines drawn indicating divisions of *Taals*.

13. **Extending or prolonging** of Notes, a dash (—) is written after the notes. One dash shows one matra time.

	1st Khand	2nd Khand	3rd Khand
Sam	Tali	Khali	Tali
×	2	0	3
Matras 1 2 3 4	5 6 7 8	9 10 11 12	13 14 15 16

14. Two, Three or Four notes in a **matra** time. These notes are combined together by a bracket under the notes i.e. SR SRG SRGM

15. **Jhala (Vamping):** To express *Jhala* normally "*J*" sign is used. But traditionally and mostly a space is mentioned (–) as *jhala* with notes.

16. **Meend:** Meend is shown by a semicircular line over the notes i.e. $\overset{\frown}{SG}$ $\overset{\frown}{SM}$ $\overset{\frown}{SP}$.

17. **Chikari:** Small (c) is written after the note. i.e. Sc, Rc,Gc.

18. **Kan Swara (Grace note):** Small letter is written in superscript by the side of the main note on the right.
    M^G P^M

19. **Prolonging, Pause or Extending the note length:** Dashes are placed after a note, one dash is fixed for one matra time.

    i.e. S—, R— —,G— —.

Format of Music on Bansuri

We have learnt a lot about the theory of music and at the same time are familiar with the fundamentals of music. In another words we now know how to play natural and flat or sharp notes on the Bansuri. But there is a great confusion when we start playing. After playing the basic notes our mind wonders what next? What should be played thereafter when we have played so called basics of music. Every instrument has its own unique features and hence every instrument has some fixed protocol according to which they are played. Our Bansuri is no exception to this rule. Here in the Bansuri there are certain things which are fixed and it is played according to that rule only. When we talk about this rule, we find out how music in produced on the Bansuri which is soothing and appealing to the audience.

The Bansuri is a classical instrument on which generally classical music is played, although light music are also played on it. When we play light music on it we follow the tune of the song or music created by the music director only. But when we talk about the Bansuri without any special reference we mean classical music only. So, lets understand how music is played on the Bansuri.

We start from "*Aalap*", which is an introduction to "*Raga*". Aalap is spread in three octaves. Here the artist shows his imagination and different permutation and combination of notes which are used in the *Raga*. After finishing it we start "*Jod*". Jod is a technique in which actual rhythm is not played but it is very much in rhythm. Different tempos are used to play the *Jod*. First of all we start with slow tempo and gradually we increase the speed and play different "*Taans*" also. At a critical rate of speed the tempo of *Jod* is so fast that it takes the form of "*Jhala*". Again this is the *Jhala* in which no rhythm is played but the *Jhala* itself is in rhythm. After finishing the *Jhala* the Tabla joins in and we play "*Vilambit* Gat". Here the artist shows his mastery over the *Raga* and pours the notes in different melodious combination. Thereafter "*Drut Gat*" is played. In *Drut Gat* the artist shows his command over the speed and tempo. Gradually increasing the speed the artist finishes with *Jhala*.

Western Notation System

The Western notation system is based on time symbols and where they are placed on the staff. These signs show both the *Swaras* and the length of time. These symbols are the notes, written on a set of 5 horizontal lines and 4 equal spaces between them called the Staff. There are two sets of the staff on which music notes are written: one for the lower tones or sounds and the other for the higher tones or sounds. The **lower tones or pitches** are represented by the **Bass** (*pronounced base*) **Staff** on which the Bass Clef Sign (𝄢) is written and the **higher tones or pitches** and **medium tones or pitches** are represented by the **Treble Staff** on which the Treble clef sign (𝄞) is written. Together these two staves make the **Grand Staff.**

The symbols of notes used in western music and their near meanings in Indian Music are given below.

Symbols of Notes		Sound Values
Whole Note or Semi-breve	𝅝	4 beats)*Matra*) of sound
Half Note or Minim	𝅗𝅥	2 beats (*Matra*) of sound
Quarter Note or Crotchet	𝅘𝅥	1 beat (*Matra*) of sound
Dotted Half Note or Dotted Minim	𝅗𝅥.	3 beats (*Matra*) of sound
Eighth Note or Quaver	𝅘𝅥𝅮	½ beat (*Matra*) of sound
16th Note or Semi-quaver	𝅘𝅥𝅯	¼ (*Matra*) beat of sound

Symbols of Notes		Sound Values
Full Tone Notes or Naturals	♮	Shudh Swaras (denoted as SRGMPDN)
Half Tone Notes or Flats	♭	Komal Swaras (denotes with line under the note: S <u>RG</u> MP <u>DM</u>)
Sharp Note	♯	Tivra Swara (denote with a vertcal line over the note; SRGṀPDN
Bass Cleff sign	𝄢	Mandra Saptaka (denote with a '•' under the note; S R G M P D N
Treble Cleff sign	𝄞	Tar saptak (denote with a '•' over the notes: S R G M P D N

Apart from the above symbols in western music the beat is also very important. In fact it is the backbone of all music. Without the beat there is no music. The beat in music is related to Time which is Space between measuring units which are numbers. Without numbers we cannot measure time or any form of measurement for that matter. Hence Time maybe defined as space between numbers. So also the beat in music which is **Equal spaces of time between numbers**. These spaces must be equal in music otherwise it is just noise. This means if we have a piece of music that has four beats

the 1st beat will be the **space** between numbers 1 and 2

the 2nd beat will be the **space** between numbers 2 and 3

the 3rd beat will be the **space** between numbers 3 and 4, and

the 4th beat will be the **space** between numbers 4 and 1.

Unlike Indian music western music does not have a **0 beat**, which is called **Khali**. Western music starts on the 1st beat.

The symbols which represent the sounds are called notes. They have sound values to them. When written on the staff, the note symbols represent the different lengths of sound, thus, making the rhythm of music. Rhythm may then be defined as the combination of all the long and short sounds in a piece of music within a specific beat. In other words the combination of all the different kinds of notes in a piece of music. There are basically four types of Rhythm from which all music is written. These are as follows:

1. A rhythm where the sound is more than one beat (single space of time) or in other words a note represents two or more beats of sound.

2. A rhythm where the sound is equal to one beat (single space of time) or a note represents one beat of sound.

3. A rhythm where the single beat (single space of time) will have two sounds which means that the beat is divided into two sounds which are equal in length.

4. A rhythm where the single beat (space of time) will have three or four or more sounds within the beat and these are also equally divided.

Western music is also divided into sections or divisions which we call Measures which are formed by vertical lines on the staff which we call Bar Lines. The beat in western music is grouped normally in double, triple, or quadruple time that is 2, 3 or 4 beats per measure. We find this in the time signature which is a set of two numbers one above the other. These numbers are normally found in the beginning of a piece of music.

Just as we speak in sentences to make sense in music we also have musical sentences which we call phrases and which normally consist of four measures of sound but which may also vary depending on the composition. These musical sentences are marked by curved lines called Slurs. These lines are found over a set of notes on the staff which indicate the phrase of music which expresses an idea. A complete sentence would normally consists of two phrases, the first called the **statement** and the second the **response**. These musical phrases or sentences usually end in a form of punctuation which we call **cadences** in music. They denote the end of a phrase.

All music is based on scales hence scales are the skeleton or backbone of any musical composition. In western music we have two basic kinds of scales - the Major scales and the Minor scales. The Minor scales are of three types - these are Natural minor, the Harmonic minor and the Melodic minor scales. Scales are built on a pattern of Tones and semitones. These tones and semitones are the distances of sounds. The semitones are the closest distance of two notes or pitches while the tones are two semitones side by side. Basing on the pattern of tones and semitones scales are identified as whether they are sharp scales or flat scales. A **sharp scale** is when the natural note of the scale is **raised** by a semitone and a **flat scale** is when the natural note of the scale is **lowered** by a semitone.

For example:
    G major the notes are G A B C D E F$^\sharp$ G
    F major the notes are F G A B$^\flat$ C D E F

All together we have about sixty scales in western music, these include all the majors and their relative minors, in all 3 forms. The *number of sharps or flats* in them we call the **key signature** of a scale. This includes the three types of minor scales as mentioned earlier. One may compare scales to multiplication tables in school which need to be learnt if we want to understand music properly. They are most essential in music learning.

Another very important aspect of western music is the skill of reading music which is most important if one is to be a good musician. For this we learn to identify **notes** on the staff, that is the lines and spaces, by the **distances** between them as they are **written on the staff,** up or down the staff. We call this Intervals between notes. We know that there are eight notes to a scale hence we number them as 1 2 3 4 5 6 7 8 or call them the eight degrees of a scale. Basing on this we identify the intervals between notes written on the lines and spaces. The following are the intervals identified.

1. Repeat - This is the interval of notes on the same line or space on the staff.

eg. Notes on the same second line or same third space.

2. Second - (Step) - The interval from a line note to a space note up or down.

eg. Notes on the 1st line and the 1st space up or notes on the 4th space and 4th line down.

3. Third - (Skip) - The interval from a line note to the next line note or from a space note to the next space note up or down.

eg. 3rd line note to 4th line note up or 2nd space note to 1st space note down.

4. Fourth - (3rd + 2nd) - The interval from a line note to a space note or space note to a line note up or down with a space and line in between.

eg. 1st line note to 2nd space note up or 4th line note to 2nd space note down.

5. Fifth - (3rd + 3rd) - The interval from a line note to a line note or space note to a space note up or down with a line or space in between.

eg. 1st line note to 3rd line note up or 3rd space note to 1st space note down.

Interval reading helps in getting the right pitch (sound) and the correct finger to play on the instrument. This skill of reading is most helpful for a smooth flowing production of sound on any instrument.

Points To Remember for Combined Notation System

Before using combined notation system the musicians should bear the following points in mind.

1. **The middle point C is fixed for every song, *Raga* or tune. The Sa or C note is compulsory. All tunes are based on the C note.**

2. **G note [P] cannot be changed into a half tone (flat) or a sharp note.**

3. **P and F cannot be omitted at a time in any *Raga*.**

The Symbol of matra on the staff notation is accepted by our combined notation system. It is equal to one *matra* time. Symbols of No. 1 and No. 2 are not used in combined notation system. The remaining fractional *matra* time symbols may be used as they are. The position of symbol of time notes in the clefs are accepted as they are.

Symbols of half tone notes (flats) and the sharp note are accepted. The symbol of extension of sound [—] is accepted for prolonging the notes, not for ending the sound. This symbol denotes one matra time. The symbol of prolonging notes for meend without dots are accepted as [ ] and for combined notes as [ ].

In the Indian Music system there are a number of taal variations which are not used in western music. Not only this, western music uses the taal with evenly spaced numbers only but in Indian music we have a number of taals which are odd and very complicated to play and understand. The notation of these taals and compositions set to these taals are naturally very hard to grasped.

There are a number of expressions such as 1.75 times of a beat, or .25 times of a beat, or 2.75 of a beat in Indian music notation system.

These expressions should be understood in Indian system only and be mastered in order to have a better command over the music of any form.

Part – 2
Bansuri –
Then & Now

Bansuri

Bansuri, the instrument of bamboo grass, is older then we know of it. Proof of its existence is found from Lord krishna's era and during the time of Buddha. True documentation is found from Buddhist pictures depicting the use of the bamboo flute around 2000 years ago and it is mentioned in the Vedas also. The Vedas mentions the bansuri as 'swaranjana', a Sanskrit word for the source of knowledge of music.

Etymologically, Bansuri is made of two words, i.e. *baans* (bamboo) + *swar* (musical note). It is a piece of seasoned bamboo having holes on its body to allow air to flow through it giving sounds of various notes. When air flows through it, it converts the air to sound that can melt the hearts of listeners.

It has been connected to its greatest player, Lord Krishna. According to legend the Bansuri produces mesmerizing melodies on Krishna's lips. Hearing his bansuri, lost cows would find their way home and damsels of the village would forget all and run to see him. He creates magic with hypnotizing sounds of the flute. Each flute player today considers Krishna as his ideal and plays the flute with his magic-sound in his mind.

The Bansuri is a very simple instrument. Unlike string instruments, it does not need tuning once it is tuned by the flute maker. However, it is Krishna's instrument and the Lord has made it deceptively simple. But yes one needs to practice well before perfecting the art of playing it.

History and Development

The Bansuri is as old as Hindu mythology. Its legend is connected to Lord Krishna and Buddhism also talk about its existence. Its mention in the '*Vedas*' establishes this fact very prominently.

In ancient scriptures, Indian Classical music is expressed in three forms, these are *Vaani* - the vocal, *Veena* the string and *Venu* the flute. This proves their existence in music. Out of these three the Bansuri, a wind instrument, was played both solo and as an accompaniment with singing.

Ever since, it has been used in folk music by various regional artists and by musical tribes of north India. Folk artists were inspired by Lord krishna and the folk culture of Vrandavan and Mathura, which is the birth place of Lord krishna. These folk artists use the Bansuri to play in various religious and cultural occasions. It is mostly used for the purpose of expressing various activities and sermons of Lord Krishna.

Initially the north Indian bansuri used in folk music playing was 10 inches long with only one octave of natural notes. But modifications took place with modern Indian musicians giving it a new status in the world of music. Many changes were already made to the bansuri when the western flute came into existence in the middle of the 20th century.

Wind instruments like the mouth organ and the bagpipes were fast taking their place when the western world made changes to the Bansuri to create western flutes of many octaves and playing styles. These flutes are the piccolo, whistle and flutes of many octaves and sizes for specialise sounds.

44

A remarkable change was made to the Indian Bansuri when the legendary player, Shri Pannalal Ghosh, adopted the dominating Classical singing style 'khayal' for the bansuri. This changed the modern history of the Bansuri in the world. Later on following the many changes, legendary Bansuri player, Pt. Hari Prasad Chaurasiya, enriched the repertoire by elements of *dhrupad alaap* and techniques as of plucked instruments in Bansuri playing.

Many versatile musicians in India then explored bansuri playing by producing all the basic elements of Hindustani music such as the *Meend* (the glide), *Gamak*, *Kan* etc. The expressions of different playing techniques were also added to it like variations in the blowing styles.

Today the Bansuri is one of the most popular, portable and easy-to-tune instrument. It has been experimentally used in many Hindi films songs as well as fusion music. Because of its tonal quality and versatility it has become a favorite among music lovers.

Wind Instruments

Classical Indian Music mentions wind instruments as 'Sushir Vadya', the instruments that produce sound because of the air pressure through them. The natural Instruments used in ancient times were flutes of various types, Shankh (sea shells) and animal horns. Later on reeds were introduced and the second type of wind instruments came into being. When air is blown it goes through the reed chamber to produce sounds of notes.

Various ancient wind Instruments are as follows:

1.   Flute (North India)

2.   Shehnai (North India)

3.   Nagaswaram (South India)

4.   Sundari (Karnataka)

5.   Mukhveena (Tamil Nadu)

6.   Narh (Rajasthan)

7.   Aigoza (Rajasthan)

8.   Pavri (Maharashtra)

9.   Pungi (Haryana)

10.   Shankh (Orissa)

11.   Thunchen (Himalayan Region)

12.   Khanglign (Himalayan Region)

13.   Mashak (Rajasthan)

14.   Surnai (Rajasthan)

15.   Bankia (Rajasthan)

16.   Khung (Manipur)

17.   Bans (Madhya Pradesh)

18.   Mohuri (Bihar)

19.   Kol (West Bengal)

20.   Ransinga (Himachal Pradesh)

21.   Limbu (Himachal Pradesh)

The second type of wind instruments are of reed Instrument. The main instrument in this catagory is the harmonium. A very popular instrument of north india. It consists of reeds and bellows to blow air inside. Other reed instruments of India are:

1.   Harmonium

2.   Nadaswaram (South India)

3.   Mouth Organ

Wind Instruments and how they look like.

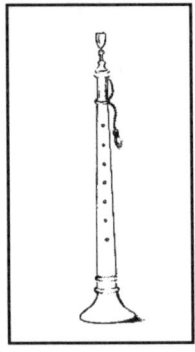

Shehnai

It is a popular wind instrument with holes on it to produce notes. It is used mostly in North Indian Music.

Nagaswaram

Popularly known as 'Mangal Vadya', it is used in Carnatic Music.

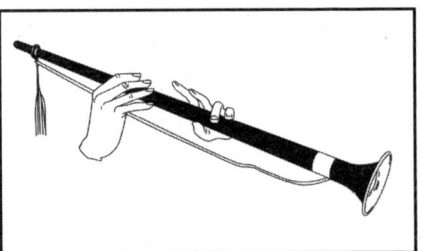

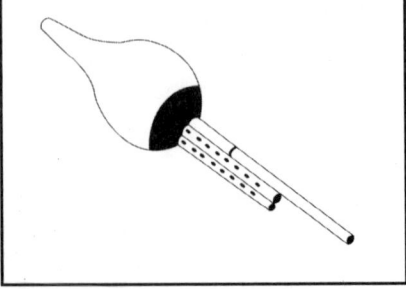

Pungi

It is an instrument used by the snake charmers. It is used in folk music also.

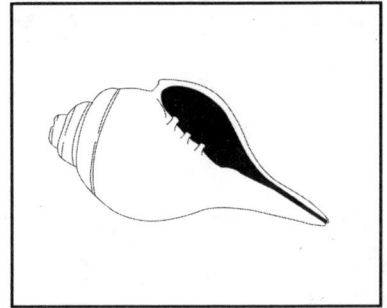

Shankh

Found in nature as a natural sea shell, it is widely used in homes during worship of Hindu Gods

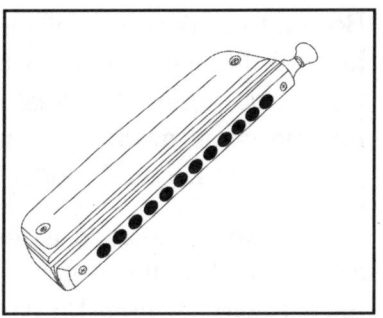

Mouth Organ

It is a popular reed instrument used in various types of music such as Jazz, Blue, Classical and many more.

Out of these wind instruments, the Bansuri is the most widely accepted and used. It may be taken as the basic instrument for the development of modern day wind instruments. It reminds us of nature as it is the instrument most close to it. Due to its simple look and extraordinary sweet and heart melting sound, it is popular among music lovers. Due to a wide range of its sound, it gets ample use in all forms of music today, be it classical or light music.

Famous Bansuri Players

Pt. Pannalal Ghosh

Pt. Pannalal Ghosh is undoubtedly the foremost exponent of the Bansuri and is credited with the introduction of it as a classical instrument from a folk instrument. Born into a musical family in 1911, he took his initial training from his father and uncles. His final rigorous training came much later under the guidance of Baba Allauddin Khan.

Pt. Ghosh worked extensively for many Indian films. He also worked as the composer of the national orchestra for All India Radio. In time he earned fame and recognition for his music and the instrument he had invented, the 34-inch long Bansuri. He even accompanied many great vocalists of the time like Ustad Faiyaz Khan and Pt. Omkarnath Thakur. Pt. Ghosh died suddenly in 1960 at the age of 49, still in his musical prime.

Pandit Hariprasad Chaurasia

Pandit Hariprasad Chaurasia is known internationally as the greatest living master of the Bansuri. He is among a few musicians who have made a conscious effort to reach out and expand the audience for classical music by popularising the Bansuri and classical music among the masses.

Born in Allahabad in year 1938 to a non-musical family of a wrestler father, Hariprasad had to learn music almost in secret. First by learning vocal music from Pt. Rajaram at the age of 15 and later, by playing the flute under the tutelage of Pt. Bholanath of Varanasi. Later in his life, while working for All India Radio, he received guidance from the reclusive Smt. Annapurna Devi (daughter of Baba Allauddin Khan).

Pt. Chaurasia is a rare combination of innovator and traditionalist. He has significantly expanded the expressive possibilities of North Indian classical flute through his masterful blowing technique. He is also associated with Hindi films as a musician along with his veteran musician friend Pt. Shiv Kumar Sharma.

The great Indian master of bansuri has won a number of prestigious awards including the Sangeet Natak Academy (1984), Padmabhushan (1992) and Padma Vibhoosan (2000).

Pandit Ragunath Seth

Pandit Ragunath Seth is one of the versatile bansuri masters and a disciple of the bansuri legend, Pt Pannalal Ghosh.

Ragunath Seth was born in Gwalior into a musical family. He was guided in his initial years by the noted composer and musicologist, Pt S N Ratanjankar.

Pt. Seth has made major contributions towards the enhancement of flute design. Pt. Seth designed a flute to play the glissando note with much ease and it has received recognition from the press and musicologists. Other established artists have imitated it as well.

As a classical artist, he has been giving performances in India and abroad for many years. He has also collaborated with jazz musicians on fusion albums. To his credit, he owns a long list of awards and commendations conferred upon him.

Pandit G.S. Sachdev

Gurbachan Singh Sachdev has gained international recognition and known as master of the bansuri. He belongs to Chandigrah. G.S. Sachdev started playing the bansuri at the age of 14. He got his training and nurture in music with some of India's greatest musicians including Vijay Raghav Rao, Ali Akbar Khan and Ravi Shankar. Today, his imagination and mastery knows no limit. He is continuing his masterly musical voyage to new dimensions.

Unlike many musicians, Sachdev has shied away from fusion. His music is normally considered as an antidote to tension, stress, fatigue and cynicism.

He performs and tours regularly in Europe, Asia and throughout North America. Over the years, he has developed the gift of communicating instantly with the audiences through his music.

N.Ramani

Padmashri Dr. N. Ramani also known as Flute Ramani, was born in 1934. She is a renowned Carnatic flautist from Tiruvarur, Tamil Nadu, India. A disciple of the legendary T. R. Mahalingam, commonly known as "Mali," who first popularised the Carnatic flute to the world of Indian music.

As a regular performer and an 'A' grade artist on All India Radio (AIR), her style and improvisations in the rendition of many compositions of Carnatic music brought her instantaneous fame from state level to national.

Ramani's contributions to the world of the Carnatic flute are immensely popular, especially the introduction of the duet flute concerts which have gained popular appraisals. She also introduced the long bass flute to increase the range in the lower octaves. In addition, she introduced the 2.5 pitch flute, which is ideal for violin and veena concerts, keeping the strict tradition of Carnatic music.

Beyond Carnatic music, her proficiency in Hindustani classical music pioneered the playing of the North Indian bansuri flute in Carnatic music concerts.

Some of her highlights include the Sangeetha Kalanidhi, awarded by the Music Academy in Chennai, Tamil Nadu, India, the Sangeetha Acharya award from Wasser College, U.S.A., the honorary citizenship status in Maryland, Ohio, U.S.A. and the Padma Shri Award from the President of India. She holds an honorary Cultural Doctorate from The World University of Arizona.

Ronu Majumdar

Ronu Majumdar is a noted flautist in the Hindustani Classical Music tradition. Born in Varanasi on June 20, 1963, Ranendranath Majumdar, popularly known as Ronu was trained under his father and later learned vocal music with the late Pt. Laxman Prasad Jaipurwale at whose behest he reverted to the flute and finally under the revered Pt. Vijay Raghav Rao.

An energetic and tireless performer, Pt Majumdar's music is rooted in the Maihar gharana which have produced musicians of eminence like Pt Ravi Shankar and Ustad Ali Akbar Khan. Apart from his concerts all over India in different music festivals, he also participated in the Festival of India in Moscow and Asiad '82 in New Delhi. He has toured extensively in Europe, the USA , Canada, Japan, Singapore, Thailand, Australia, and the Middle East.

His speciality is the "Shank Bansuri". A three-feet long flute of his own design, which adds extra range for the lower scales. Pt. Majumdar is also known for a number of collaborations and jugalbandis with other leading instrumentalists. An innovative composer, he has also composed several pieces in a fusion of Hindustani classical with other forms of music, particularly Western Classical Music, including the projects Carrying Hope (Music Today), A Traveller's Tale, Song of Nature (Magnasound), Kal Akela Kahan (Plus Music).

The list of masters who contributed a lot to the cause of bansuri is unending, but as a matter of tribute, we hereby mention some of the prominent names from the field of Bansuri. These are:

*	Bari Siddiqui	* Sikkil Mala Chandrasekar
*	Milind Date	* Thiagarajan Ramani
*	Vijay Raghav Rao	* Tiruchy L. Saravanan
*	T. Viswanathan	* Harsh Wardhan

Part – 3
Know The Bansuri

Various Types of Bansuri

The Bansuri can be classified based on types and then within these types it is further classified based on lengths and octaves.

The two different styles of playing the bansuri gives them a separate identity. These two different types of Bansuri based on their playing styles are:

1. Fipple of straight holding Bansuri and

2. Transverse of side holding Bansuri.

1. Fipple or straight holding Bansuri

The straight holding Bansuri is a technique found in folk styles but seldom used for serious music. The process of blowing is very simple. The player puts the blowing piece of the flute between his lips and blows. This is usually considered an easy technique because of the absence of any embouchure. It limits the 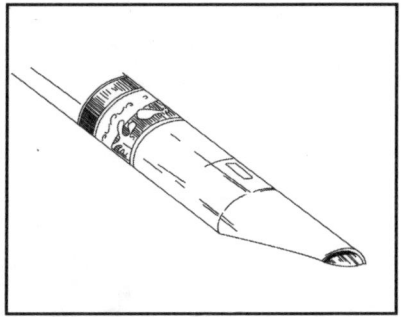 flexibility of the instrument. This style of flute may be called many things in India such as *bansi*, bansuri, *murali*, *venu* and many more. Being known as a folk instrument, it does not require extensive learning techniques. It is easy to hold and play.

2. Transverse or side holding Bansuri

The transverse type of Bansuri is well known in the Indian Classical music scene. This is a long bamboo with six or seven holes on it. The blowing part is another hole with a reed like air-chamber to convert the blown air to musical sound. This is the preferred flute for classical music because the embouchure gives added flexibility and control. The Player here can use many techniques in embouchure like tongue rolling, blocking and blow stopping to create effects like *meend*, *gamak*, *kan* etc. The player keeps it horizontally from his mouth and downward towards the ground while playing.

This type of bansuri comes in various sizes and variety. The traditional bansuri is of bamboo, but these days we also find metal bansuris made of Steel, brass and other material.

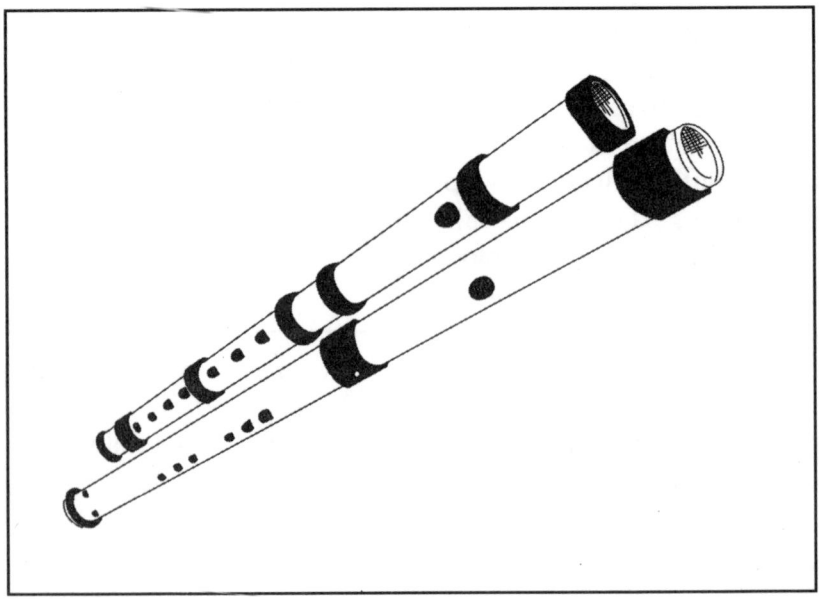

Bansuri on the basis of Pitch

Modern day bansuri comes in various sizes according to pitch and octaves. One bansuri cannot be used for producing different octave notes, that is why different bansuris of different notes are available to play. Some bansuris are of lower octaves while others are for higher octaves just like the Harmonium, which is played with different keys by different people.

Each bansuri has its own note, on the basis of which the octave is played around that note. Small bansuris produce higher octave notes while long bansuris produce lower octave notes. Based on this theory eight types of modern bansuris are found. These are:

Bansuri on the basis of Notes of Pitch

Bansuri No.	Length	Note	Octave
A	34	Dha	Higher
B	38	Ni	Higher
C	39	Sa	Middle
D	40	Ni	Lower
F	41	Dha	Lower
G	42	Pa	Lower
A Double	78	Ga	Double Lower
C Double	64	Sa	Double Lower
F Double	54	Ma	Double Lower

Parts of a Bansuri

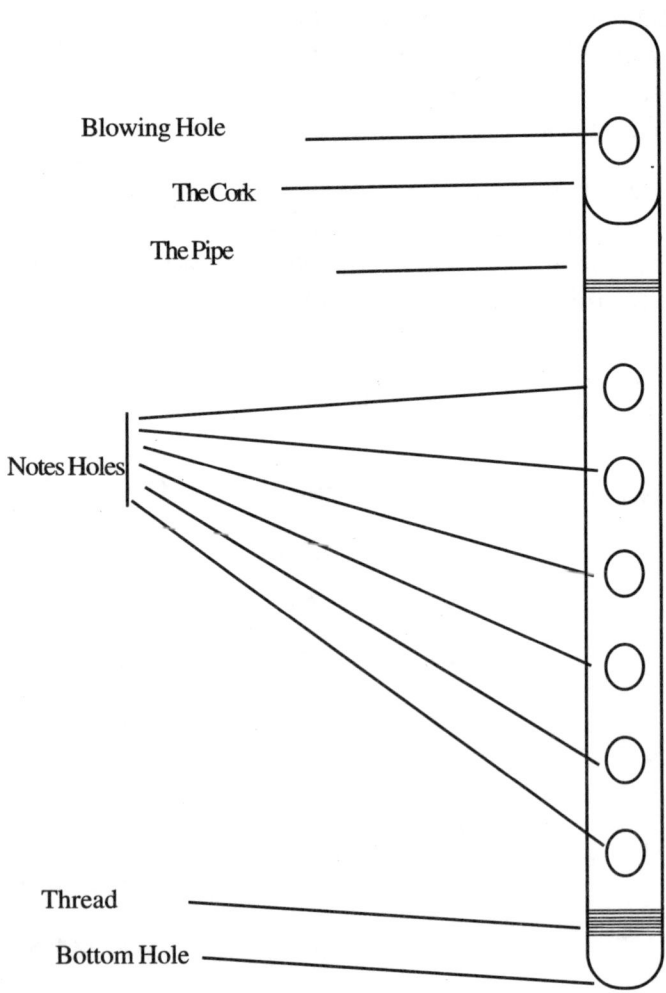

Blowing Hole

The Cork

The Pipe

Notes Holes

Thread

Bottom Hole

Parts of a Bansuri

1. The Pipe (*Nali or Dandi*)

The body of a bansuri is generally made from reed, cane, bamboo or bronze. It contains various holes as required. The holes of the flute should be in one straight line. The blowing hole, on the top of all holes, through which the air is blown, should be a bit bigger than the other 6 holes. The inner part of the flute must be hollow and soft. A cork piece is fixed on the end of the main hole where the lips blow air. This cork is meant for producing sound. The inner part should be plane and soft so that it may not become an obstacle allowing air up the cork freely.

2. The cork

This is a very important part of the flute because the fineness of the sound depends upon a well adjusted cork. The prime function of the cork in a flute is to divert blown air towards the holes and hence convert to sounds. It is fixed to the upper portion of the bigger hole through which air is blown. If the cork is not well adjusted at the proper place, it is very difficult to play on it. Hence the smoothness of the inner part of the flute is very essential. The *Murli* type flute is not fitted with a piece of cork. A slanting cut wooden piece is placed in such a way that air from the mouth strikes directly on the body of the flute.

3. Blowing hole (*Mukhya Randhra*)

This is an important part of a Bansuri placed on the upper part of the body used for blowing air. Blowing hole technically known as the embouchure in bansuri playing. The blowing hole is a prominent part of a transverse Bansuri as there is a whistle hole in the fipple bansuri.

4. Note Holes (*Swar Chidra*)

These are six holes on top of the body. These holes are where the notes are played on the Bansuri; also known as finger holes. The fingers over these holes produces various notes on the bansuri. All these holes have the capacity to produce upto 12 notes of an octave depending upon the note which the Bansuri has been made on.

5. Bottom Hole (*Garbha randhra*)

The main hole at the bottom of the body is known as the bottom hole. It plays an important role in bansuri playing. The bottom hole is not blocked while playing. This hole plays the note **Pa** of the octave. But if we manipulate the notes of the bansuri the bottom hole will change accordingly. The pitch will remain the same only the name of the note will be changed.

6. Thread (*Rassi*)

The body of the bansuri has some marks of cracks on it. This is one prominent feature of the bamboo. Rassi is the twine that is wound around the bansuri to prevent it from cracking. This thread is tied on the body of the bansuri in order to prevent it from cracking due to fluctuating weather conditions. A tightly tied bansuri with ropes ensures that no cracking appears on the bansuri. It keeps it intact and safe for a longer time.

Making of a Bansuri

The Bansuri is made from the Bamboo which is found in abundance in nature. The Bamboo stick differs in density, thickness and internal diameter hence it is difficult to find a uniform piece of bamboo stick to prepare a flute which is perfect in all aspects. Usually one starts making a flute with any bamboo stick but the effect on the character and tone of the instrument is judged by experience.

Bansuri is made by hand. For this the ratio of length vs diameter, number of knots and thickness of the bamboo is kept in mind for a desired scale. The bamboo is then cut to a length slightly longer than what is finally required and the knots are removed. After this the blowing hole is made by burning the bamboo with a hot iron rod. A cork is fixed inside the tube near the blowing hole so that the main note and its octave can be played with maximum ease. Measurements are made and the bamboo is again cut to achieve the correct pitch. Similarly, other holes are made on the bamboo.

The next most complex process is that of tuning the bansuri. It is tuned by adjusting the size of the holes. The holes can only be widened and not shortened, so any error would waste the entire bansuri. This is where the skill of a seasoned craftsman is required. They are tuned only to the pure diatonic scale. After that it is washed and dipped in a mixture of various oils and antiseptic solution for over 24 hours. After which the oil is allowed to drain for another 24 hours.

The bansuri is now ready to be played with some final touches added.

Tips to Maintain a Bansuri

Tip 1 Bansuris, unlike Western metal flutes, do not need any specific maintenance as long as they are played regularly and kept in a relatively moist climate. E.g. it is unnecessary to wipe the inside after playing.

Tip 2 Never keep a bansuri in a hot dry place for a longer time. Otherwise the inside might swell due to its sudden exposure to the moisture of the breath and thus cause the bamboo to crack.

Tip 3 Avoid playing in cold ambient conditions. Warm breath going in the bore will rapidly expand the insides with the outer surface remaining cold and unexpended, leading to development of a crack.

Tip 4 Avoid exposing to extreme temperatures.

Tip 5 Take care not to knock or drop your Bansuri against any hard surface as bamboo though being a very resilient and strong material is susceptible to developing cracks due to its uni-directional fiber orientation.

Tip 6 Ensure that your Bansuri is protected by stringing/ bindings at both the ends. Threading is vital for a long and healthy life of your bamboo flute.

Tip 7 If you ever notice threading/binding coming off your bansuri, fix it right away. Thread it again or if you can't, apply 4-5 rounds of tape around in place of the lost threading till you are able to have thread binding done.

Tip 8 In the long run, oiling helps to protect the bansuri against the effects of repeated moisture and humidity fluctuations.

Part - 4
Playing The Bansuri

Positions For Playing

Position 1: Sitting on ground.

This is the ancient position of sitting, also known as the traditional Indian sitting position. Here the player crosses both legs inside as crossing one over the other. By keeping the left leg bend inside first followed by the right leg, gives an easy and comfortable position to the player. The Back should always remain straight. One should hold the Bansuri in the hand to play. The Bansuri should be horizontally held with the bottom hole pointing towards the ground. The hands are positioned parallel to the body with fingers spread freely over the body on the holes.

Position 2: Sitting on an unarmed chair.

Here the player picks an unarmed chair for himself and settles down comfortably on it. The chair should be tall enough for the feet to rest on the ground firmly and tall enough to keep the back straight in an upright position. The player holds the bansuri horizontally and plays by placing the fingers freely moving over the holes. This is a concert playing technique, where notes are to be followed accompanying other instruments.

Position 3: Standing Position

This is a free style of playing where a person can swing along with the mood of playing. The western style of flute playing is generally this style. The standing position is easier in western style of flute such as the piccolo where the meend and *gamaks* are not used and we get keys for all the tones and semitones over the flute itself.

Blowing on Bansuri

Blowing is the most important technique of Bansuri playing. It is very essential to produce a clean tone out of your transverse Bansuri. That is done with a simple trick of 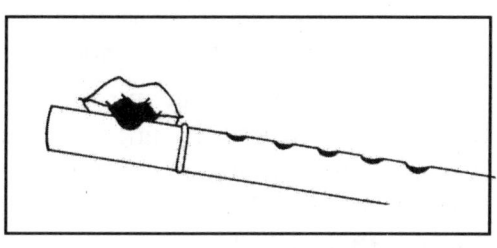 sideblowing over the blow hole. One can try and practice on the cap of a pen when you hold the cap near your lower lip on the opening and blow infront of the mouth of the cap, letting half the air go inside and half outside. This will sound like a whistle.

Blowing into the bansuri is just the same as into a pen-cap. Try blowing into the blow hole to get a tone out of it. This may take a sometime for beginners but it is the prime step to bansuri playing. Keep trying to blow in air till you start getting a sound from it comfortably. Remember always that getting the sound from your bansuri is not possible by blowing straight into the hole. You have to blow at an angle in such a way that some portion of the air goes inside the flute and some of it goes out.

The next step after you get the sound is to practice it till you are able to produce a sound for a longer duration. Practice breathing out for a longer time, up to 10-20 seconds then blow into the flute to get the sound for a longer time. This helps by giving time to practice the fingers over the finger holes.

Beginners are advised to practice the sitting, blowing and the fingering, step by step so that they have good control over one aspect of playing before getting into another.

Positions of Fingers on Bansuri

After one learns to blow properly for a longer sound, the positions of fingers over the finger holes is to be understood.

The Bansuri is held in an oblique position. The hands should be positioned so that the fingers are placed on the holes of the flute and the thumbs are rested opposite to the fingers, i.e. below the holes. The three fingers of the left hand and three fingers of the right hand covers the holes of the flute. One can cover the last hole with the little finger. The tips of the fingers should be placed on the hole in such a way that they cover it entirely and allow the air to pass out only through the outlet from which the sound is to be produced.

There are two popular holding styles of bansuri:

Style 1: In this style, the holes are covered by the tips of the fingers. By using the finger tips to close the holes. The right hand can be stretched to cover the seventh hole of the bansuri.

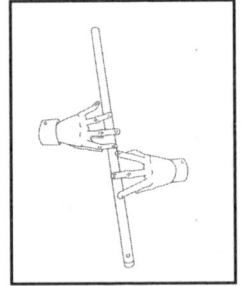

Style 2: In this style, the flat portion of fingers, not the tips, are used to cover the holes. In order to understand this style better, role over the following image to see what portions of the fingers are used to cover which holes. Also, keep in mind that the lines on your fingers are not over the holes as that will lead to leakage of air.

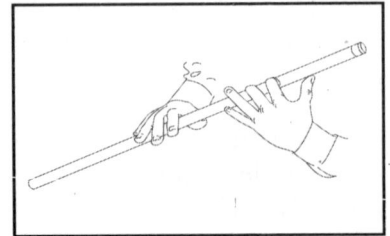

Tips While Playing the Bansuri

ॐ ═══════════════════════════════ ♋

Now that we have the sitting postures for playing the bansuri it is your choice to select any of them according to your convenience. Keep the instrument in the proper way according to your posture choice. Now there are some important tips to follow while playing.

TIP 1

Keep the Bansuri in the proper position and apply firm pressure on the tips of fingers over the holes so that they keep the air in. Or the right hand fingers over the holes instead of the tips.

TIP 2

Move the fingers in a manner that when removing one finger from a hole, the pressure of the fingers on the other holes will not decrease.

TIP 3

The pressure of air blown should increase when ascending and decrease when descending.

TIP 4

When practicing the pressure of air and the stroke of the tongue should keep pace with one another and gradually try to play all the notes in one breath.

TIP 5

When one note is played twice, such as SS RR GG etc., it should be played with the stroke of the tongue.

TIP 6

Use the tongue stroke on the basis of the tune.

TIP 7

The beat and rhythm should always be kept in mind. When practicing the stroke of the root is essential at every matra beat.

TIP 8

For half tone notes, either change the position of the notes or play them keeping the holes half open. Initially changing the position of the notes is a better method.

TIP 9

Keep the bansuri cork fitted and clean from inside. Some players use oil to smoothen the inner part of the bansuri to keep it in perfect tune.

TIP 10

Practice for about half an hour everyday and try to get the chance to play in the company of seasoned players.

Part - 5
Notes on Bansuri

Playing Basic Swaras

The first thing to be done to produce music on any instrument is by learning how to play basic notes on it. We, therefore, learn here how to produce the basic notes *(Swaras)* on the Bansuri.

There are 7 natural notes or *Shuddha swars*, as it happens in music, played on the Bansuri by blowing and finger placements. All the *Shuddha* and *Teevra* or *Komal swaras* are produced by blocking or opening the holes completely or partially. Naturally, the finger placement is very important in order to master over the art of playing bansuri. The art of finger placement should be mastered by the beginner to gain fluency in playing the notes in a rhythmic pattern. After practicing the prolonged sound by blowing and finger placement over the fingerholes one must start producing notes properly to play the rhythmical patterns and *Ragas*.

All *Shuddha* and *Teevra swaras* are produced on the bansuri by maneuvering the pressure of the fingers on the hole and allowing the cavity to pass the air as required. If one lets his finger to allow the hole to be opened fully, all *Shuddha swaras*, except *Teevra* **Ma**, is produced. *Teevra* **Ma** is the only note which is played by letting the hole to be opened fully.

The technique of playing *komal swara* requires practice. While playing the *komal swaras* on the Bansuri, the finger requires partially to be lifted from the hole to stop the air to completely flow out. Partially covered hole would lead to distortion of the sound and helps producing *komal swaras*.

75

The technique of producing all the 4 komal and 1 *tivra* *swar* is mentioned below.

Shuddha Swaras

1. **Sa :** The first note is Sa. Sa note of the medium Octave is produced by blowing air from the mouth and keeping 3 holes from below open.

2. **Re:** The second note is Re. Re note of the medium Octave is produced by blowing air from the mouth and keeping 4 holes from below open.

3. **Ga:** The third note is Ga. Ga note of the medium Octave is produced by blowing air from mouth and keeping 5 holes below open.

4. **Tivra Ma:** The fourth note is *tivra* Ma. Ma note of the medium Octave is produced by blowing air from the mouth and keeping all the holes open.

5. **Pa:** The fifth note is Pa. Pa note of the medium Octave is produced by blowing air from the mouth and keeping all the holes closed.

6. **Dha:** The sixth note is Dha. Dha note of the medium Octave is produced by blowing air from the mouth and keeping one hole from below open.

7. **Ni:** The seventh note is Ni. Ni note of the medium Octave is produced by blowing air from the mouth and keeping 2 holes from below open.

8. **Sa:** The eighth note of the octave is *Sa*, which is produced by blowing air with double force and keeping 3 holes from below open as discussed earlier.

Shuddha Ma : Shuddha Ma of the middle octave is played on the Bansuri by blowing air and keeping all the holes of the bottom open but the first finger of the left hand slightly raised over the hole to allow air to pass slightly.

Komal Swaras

Komal or flat notes are extensively used in the Indian Music System. They are the semi-tones of their respective natural notes. These notes add to the beauty of music, on the one hand and completes the spectrum of music, on the other.

Initially, it may appear a bit difficult in producing these notes on the bansuri, but with constant effort and practice one can master the art. While full tone notes or the natural notes are produced on the bansuri by letting the air to pass through the whole hole, the semi-tones or the *komal swaras* are produced by blocking the holes partially. Here we understand the technique in detail.

Komal Re

Komal Re note of the medium Octave is produced by blowing air from the mouth and keeping 3 holes from below open, as played to produce Sa, whereas the third finger allows the hole to remain half open or partially blocked. That means finger will cover the hole but slightly raised to let some air pass from it.

Komal Ga

Komal Ga note of the medium Octave is produced by blowing air from the mouth and leaving 4 holes from below open and the 2nd finger keeps the hole half open or partially blocked to let some air pass from it.

Komal Dha

Komal Dha note of the medium Octave is produced by blowing air from the mouth and blocking all the holes of the bansuri but third finger of the right hand allows some air to pass from the hole by blocking it partially. That means the finger will cover the hole but slightly raised to let some air pass from it.

Komal Ni

Komal Ni note of the medium Octave is produced by blowing air from the mouth and keeping 2 holes from below open and the first finger of the right hand blocks the hole partially and allow only some air to pass.

Thus we have seen how to produce these semi-tone notes on a bansuri. Practice these well in order to gain a firm grip over these techniques and to play the bansuri well.

Notes Placement on Bansuri

Most of the natural musical instruments in India are made to imitate the human voice. That is why they have the capacity to operate in all three octaves as in singing.

Actually the bansuri exists in many pitch and scale. The player chooses it according to his choice and ability of the instrument to harmonize with the other musical instruments. Generally, for solo performances the player prefers the bansuri in the scale **C** of the middle octave. But, sometimes, for accompaniment the bansuri of higher or lower octave may be used.

There might be a possibility that a player cannot arrange another bansuri of different scale. For this we can maneuver the tone and pitch of the instrument by shifting the note placement. For example, we take note '**pa**' as scale '**C**' and simultaneously all other notes of the octave will change accordingly to complete the octave.

Based on the same theory the positions of notes can be fixed on the bansuri. But for playing the Bansuri on distant octaves, different bansuris are used. These bansuris, as we have discussed before comes with specialised notes based. Smaller the length of the bansuri higher the octave and longer the bansuri lower the octave. Great musicians such as Pt. Hariprasad chaurasiya also keeps Bansuris of various different notes while performing at concerts to give each Raga and composition a special feel.

Given below:

The chart of various Notes Position of Bansuri.

1	S	2	S	3	S	4	S
2	R	3	R	4	R	5	R
3	G	4	G	5	G	6	G
4	M	5	M	6	M	7	M
5	P	6	P	7	P	1	P
6	D	7	D	1	D	2	D
7	N	1	N	2	N	3	N

Double force blowing

1	S	2	S	3	S	4	S

Tips For Buying a Bansuri

The Bansuri is not a costly instrument as compared to other instruments in India and abroad. It is made from the naturally existing bamboo sticks and then treated to suit the choice of the musicians. Therefore, from the cost point of view it is not very dear, but according to its usefulness its importance and utility is immense. This aspect makes purchasing bansuri a little difficult. Any ordinary buyer maybe deceived by its appearance but it is the correct tuning that is important. Therefore the following points should be kept in mind when purchasing a bansuri.

TIP 1

Normally a new buyer is attracted to the finishing of a bansuri but remember it is the sound quality and not the appearance that is important. A buyer should take note of its tonal quality and pitch.

TIP 2

The quality of a bamboo used in the bansuri is very important. A Bansuri with seasoned wood should be preferred only because this type of wood is resistant against the weather effects and lasts longer.

TIP 3

The tuning of a bansuri should be perfect in order to produce the notes correctly and with maximum ease.

TIP 4

The price and size are other aspects to be kept in mind. Initially a cheaper bansuri will do because there is danger of wear and tear in a beginner's hand. Later on when one has mastered the art, a new and better quality could be purchased.

TIP 5

The length of the Bansuri that suits the buyer should be kept in mind. Consult a good teacher when selecting a Bansuri size for you. Playing a long Bansuri at the initial stage may be a bit difficult as blowing on it takes some extra effort.

These are not the standard rule to be quoted. As a matter of fact these are only guidelines to help a new buyer in selecting a good Bansuri. But, while purchasing the instrument one should apply his or her on wisdom. There are different circumstances when you purchase any thing.

Playing Songs on Bansuri

There are a number of Hindi film songs played on the Bansuri. Here we are giving some of the selected songs to practice on the bansuri on the basis of this book.

Song 1. Jab koi Baat Bigar jaaye

Film name : Jurm   Singer : Kumar Sanu & S. Sargam
Music by Rajesh Roshan   Lyrics by Indeevar
                    Beat : Kahrava

1	2	3	4	5	6	7	8	1	2	3	4	5	6	7	8
S	S	S	S	S	S	S	S	S	S	S	S	Jab	S	ko	i
D	–	P	M	R	–	S	N	D	–	–	–	M	–	M	M
baa	S	t	bi	ga	d	ja	S	ye	S	S	S	ja	b	ko	i
D	–	–	D	P	P	M	–	D	–	–	–	P	D	P	M
mu	sh	kil	S	pa	d	ja	S	ye	S	S	S	S	S	tu	m
P	P	D	–	P	P	M	–	R	–	–	–	–	–	R	M
de	S	na	S	sa	S	th	me	ra	S	S	S	O	hum	S	na
P	–	D	–	P	–	M	M	M	R	–	–	S	R	–	M
wa	S	S	S	S	S	S	S	z	S	S	na	ko	S	i	S
R	M	–	–	–	–	–	–	R	–	–	M	M	–	M	–
Hai	S	S	na	ko	S	i	S	tha	S	S	zi	n	da	gi	S
D	–	–	D	P	–	M	–	D	–	–	P	–	D	P	M

84

1	2	3	4	5	6	7	8	1	2	3	4	5	6	7	8
me	s	s	tu	mhaa	s	re	si	va	s	s	s	s	s	tu	m
P	–	–	D	P	–	M	M	M	R	–	–	–	–	R	M
de	s	na	s	sa	s	th	me	ra	s	s	s	O	hum	s	na
P	–	D	–	P	–	M	M	M	R	–	–	S	N	–	D
waa	s	s	s	s	s	s	s	Z	s	s	s	s	s	tu	m
R	M	–	–	–	–	–	–	R	–	–	–	–	–	R	M
de	s	na	s	sa	s	th	me	ra	s	s	s	O	hum	s	s
P	–	D	–	P	–	M	M	M	R	–	–	S	N	–	–
na	waa	s	s	s	s	s	s	Z	s	s	s	s	s	s	s
D	PD	M	–	–	–	–	–	–	–	–	–	–	–	–	–

PARA I

1	2	3	4	5	6	7	8	1	2	3	4	5	6	7	8
s	s	s	s	s	s	ho	oo	chan	s	d	ni	ja	b	ta	k
Ṁ	–	–	–	–	–	Ṡ	N	Ṡ	–	Ṡ	N	Ṡ	Ṡ	Ṡ	N
raa	s	s	t	s	de	s	ta	hai	s	ha	r	ko	s	i	s
Ṡ	–	–	Ṡ	–	Ṡ	–	Ṡ	Ṡ	–	Ṡ	Ṙ	Ṙ	–	Ṡ	N
saa	s	s	th	s	tu	m	ma	gar	s	s	an	dhe	s	roọ	s
N	–	–	N	–	Ṙ	–	Ṙ	Ṙ	–	–	Ṙ	Ṙ	–	Ṙ	G
s	me	s	s	s	s	na	s	s	chho	d	na	s	me	s	ra
–	Ġ	Ṙ	Ṡ	–	–	Ṡ	P	–	P	P	Ṡ	–	Ṡ	N	ND
haa	s	s	th	s	s	s	s	ss	ss	ss	s	s	s	s	s
D	–	–	–	–	–	–	–	MD	SR	SD	S	–	Ṃ	Ḍ	S

1	2	3	4	5	6	7	8	1	2	3	4	5	6	7	8
S	S	S	S	Jab	S	ko	i	baa	S	t	bi	ga	d	ja	S
MD	SR	SD	S	M	–	M	M	D	–	–	D	P	P	M	–
ye	S	S	S	ja	b	ko	i	mu	sh	kil	S	pad	S	jaa	S
D	–	–	–	P	D	P	M	P	P	D	–	P	–	M	–
ye	S	S	S												
R	–	–	–												

Para II

wafadari ki vo rasme nibhayenge hum tum kasme

ek bhi saans zindagi ki jab tak hai apne bas me

Jab koi baat bigad jaaye.............

Para III

Dil ko mere hua yakee hum pehle bhi mile kahee

silsila ye sadiyo ka koi aaj ki baat nahi

jab koi baat higad jaaye.............

Song2: Kal ho na ho

Film name : kal ho na ho   Singer : Sonu nigam
Music by Shankar,ehsan & loy   Lyrics by Javed Akhtar

Beat : Kahrava

1	2	3	4	5	6	7	8	1	2	3	4	5	6	7	8
–	–	–	–	–	–	–	–	–	–	–	–	–	–	–	–
Ṙ	–	–	–	Ġ	–	–	–	P	PṠ	PS	GP	P	PṠ	PS	GP

s	ss	ss	ss	s	ss	ss	ss	har	gha	di	ba	dal	ra	hi	hai
P	PṠ	PS	GP	P	PṠ	PS	GP	Ṡ	N	Ṡ	N	Ṡ	N	ṠG	Ṙ

roo	p	zi	nda	gi	s	s	s	chha	av	hai	ka	bhi	ka	bhi	hai
N	D	N	D	N	–	–	–	Ṡ	Ṅ	Ṡ	N	Ṡ	N	ṠG	Ṙ

dhoo	p	zi	nda	gi	har	pal	ya	han	s	s	s	s	jee	bhar	ji
N	D	N	D	N	P	D	Ṡ	D	–	–	–	–	M	P	D

yo	s	s	s	s	jo	hai	sa	ma	s	s	s	s	kal	ho	naa
P	–	–	–	–	P	D	Ṡ	D	–	–	–	PM	M	N	D

ho	s	s	s	s	s	s	s	(REPEAT)							
P	–	–	–	–	–	–	–								

PARA I

s	ss	s	s	s	ss	s	s	s	chaa	he	jotu	mhe	s	poo	re
Ṙ	PṠ	–	–	D	NṠ	Ṡ	–	DP	N	Ṡ	MĠ	Ṙ	–	N	D

dil	s	se	s	s	s	s	s	s	mil	ta	hai	woh	s	mu	sh
N	–	Ṡ	–	Ṙ	–	D	–	–	NṠ	M	G	Ṙ	–	N	D

kil	s	se	s	s	s	ss	s	ss	ai	sa	jo	ko	s	i	ka
N	–	Ṡ	D	P	–	DP	D	NR	NṠ	M	Ġ	Ṙ	–	N	D

hin	s	hai	s	s	s	s	s	s	bas	vo	hi	sab	s	se	ha
N	–	Ṡ	–	D	–	Ṙ	–	Ṡ	NṠ	M	G	ṘR	–	N	D

87

1	2	3	4	5	6	7	8	1	2	3	4	5	6	7	8
seen	s	hai	s	s	us	haa	th	ko	s	s	ss	s	tum	thaa	m
N	–	Ṡ	D	P	P	D	Ṡ	D	–	–	N̲D̲	M	M	P	D
lo	s	s	ss	s	vo	mehe	r	ba	s	s	s	s	kal	ho	na
P	–	–	S̲G̲	R	P	D	Ṡ	D	–	–	P	M	M	N̲	D
ho	s	s	s	s	har	pal	ya	ha	s	s	s	s	ji	bhar	ji
P	–	–	S̲G̲	R	P	D	Ṡ	D	–	–	P	M	M	N̲	D
yo	s	s	s	s	jo	hai	sa	ma	s	s	s	s	kal	s	ho
P	–	–	–	–	P	D	Ṡ	Ṡ̲R̲	D	–	P	M	M	–	N̲
s	na	ho	s	s	s	s	s	s	s	s	s	s	s	s	s
–	D	P	–	–	–	–	–	–	–	–	–	–	–	–	–

Para II

palko ke le ke saaye aansu koi jo aaye

lakh sambhalo pagal dil ko dil dhadke hi jaaye

par soch lo is pal hai jo, vo dastan kal ho na ho

har ghadi ....

Notes

Notes

Notes

PANKAJ PUBLICATIONS

Suggested Readings on Wind Instruments

Learn to Play on Flute

ISBN: 81-87155-33-7

A Bestseller book of the popular 'Learn to Play series', talks about Learning the worlds' favourite instrument in detail. Pictorial details of handling, postures and tuning the instrument for the comfort of eavery learner. A sure pick for the a learner.

Sitar - Learn & PLay

Hindi   - ISBN: 81-87155-

Book in HINDI & ENGLISH languages explaining the techniques of learning and playing the Bansuri like a pro. Color pictures with detail explanation.

PANKAJ PUBLICATIONS

- *Presents* -

Practice books for music Learners

SELECTED HINDI SONGS
WITH NOTATIONS & CHORDS

The series presents the songbooks in the form of collection of songs for early musicians to practice. The notations with the songs let learners practice to play the songs on Indian Notation System and on chords. The series has collection of songs in Hindi, as well as their romanized version for easy readability for English speaking people.

PANKAJ PUBLICATIONS

Learn to Play on... Series

Book Name	ISBN
Learn to play on Tabla Vol-1	81-87155-00-0
Learn to play on Tabla Vol-2	81-87155-01-9
Learn to play on Harmonium	81-87155-22-1
Learn to play on Flute	81-87155-33-7
Learn to play on Sitar	81-87155-14-0
Learn to play on Violin	81-87155-46-9
Learn to play on Veena	81-87155-47-7
Learn to play on Guitar	81-87155-15-9
Learn to play on Mouth Organ	81-87155-03-5
Learn to play on Bongo-Congo	81-87155-68-X
Guitar Chords	81-87155-16-7
Indian Dances for Beginners	81-87155-02-7
MIND OVER FINGERS	81-87155-80-9
Distinction! in Music Theory Exam	81-87155-94-9

For Information or to Order,

Please visit our website: **www.pankajmusic.com**
or Email us at: contact@pankajmusic.com
or simply write to: **Pankaj Publications, 3, Regal Building, Sansad Marg, New Delhi - 1100 01.**